The Spooks Step Out

"Umansky sustains our interest, and a consistently excellent level of writing, right to the poem's fine (and suprising) conclusion."

The Independent

"I read this to 115 Year 5's at an end of term assembly and they were so keen I had to read it twice. Powerful stuff indeed."

Books for Keeps

"Children who like vampires and funny, spooky tales will love it."

Times Educational Supplement

The Spooks Step Out

KAYE UMANSKY
Illustrated by Keren Ludlow

A Dolphin
Paperback

For James – K.U.
To Tom and Josh – K.L.

First published in Great Britain in 1997
Published in paperback in 1997
by Orion Children's Books
a division of the Orion Publishing Group Ltd
Orion House
5 Upper St Martin's Lane
London WC2H 9EA

This edition published in 2006 for Index Books Limited

A CIP catalogue record for this book is available
from the British Library

Printed in Great Britain by Clays Ltd, St Ives plc

It was midnight in the fairground.

There was nobody in sight.

The gates were locked securely, with a bolt.

The horses on the roundabout

Had knocked off for the night,

And the Ferris Wheel had rumbled to a halt.

5

The swings were hanging motionless.

They did not even squeak,

Suspended from their gaily painted posts.

Then - suddenly - the Ghost Train door

Swung open with a crrreeeaaak . . .

And out into the moonlight stepped -

The Ghosts!

The first out was the Skeleton,

Long and lean of limb.

His bones beneath the moon were white

as snow.

He was followed by the Mummy.

There was no mistaking him.

He was tightly bandaged up, from head

to toe.

9

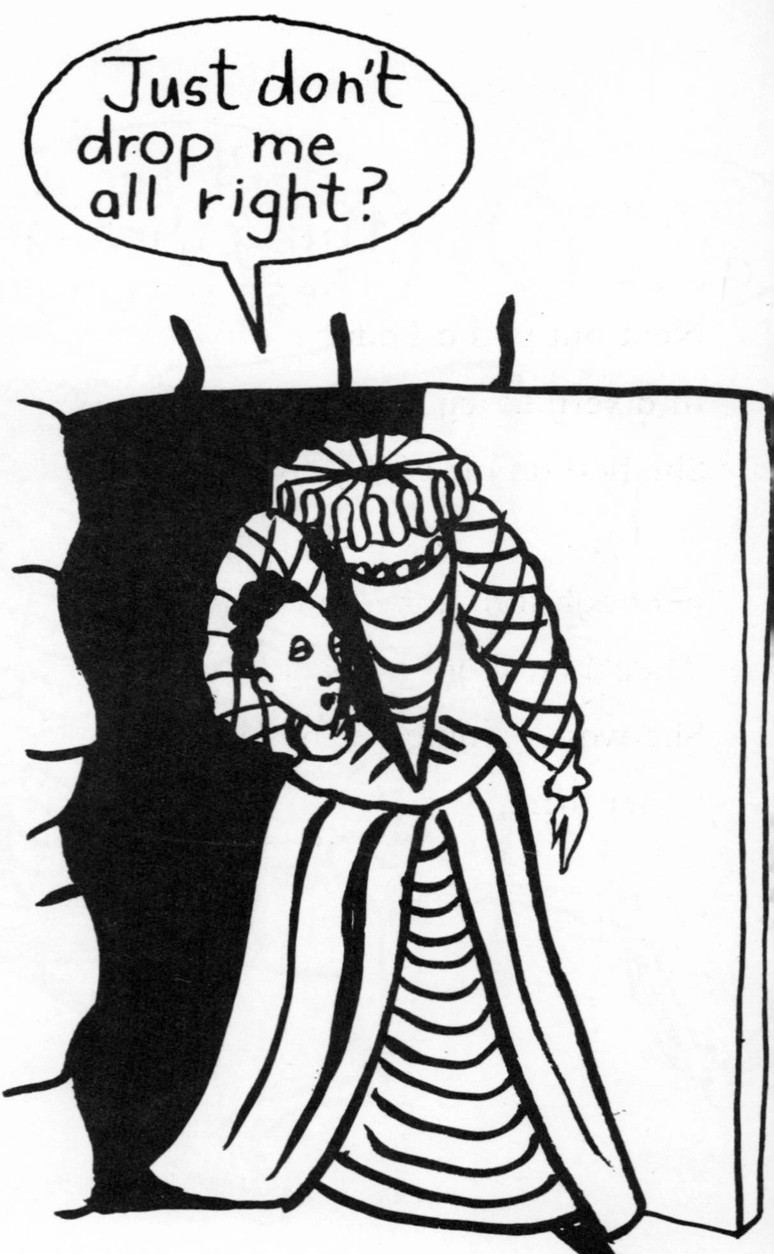
Just don't drop me all right?

Next out was a Lady
In a very fancy frock –
She had an air of dignity and charm,

(Though if anyone had seen her
They'd have got a nasty shock –
She was carrying her head beneath
   her arm!)

And last of all, a tiny Ghost

Came flapping into view,

"Hey, hang about, you rotters! Wait for me!

It isn't fair to leave me there!

You'd better take me too,

I'll report you to the R.S.P.C.G!"

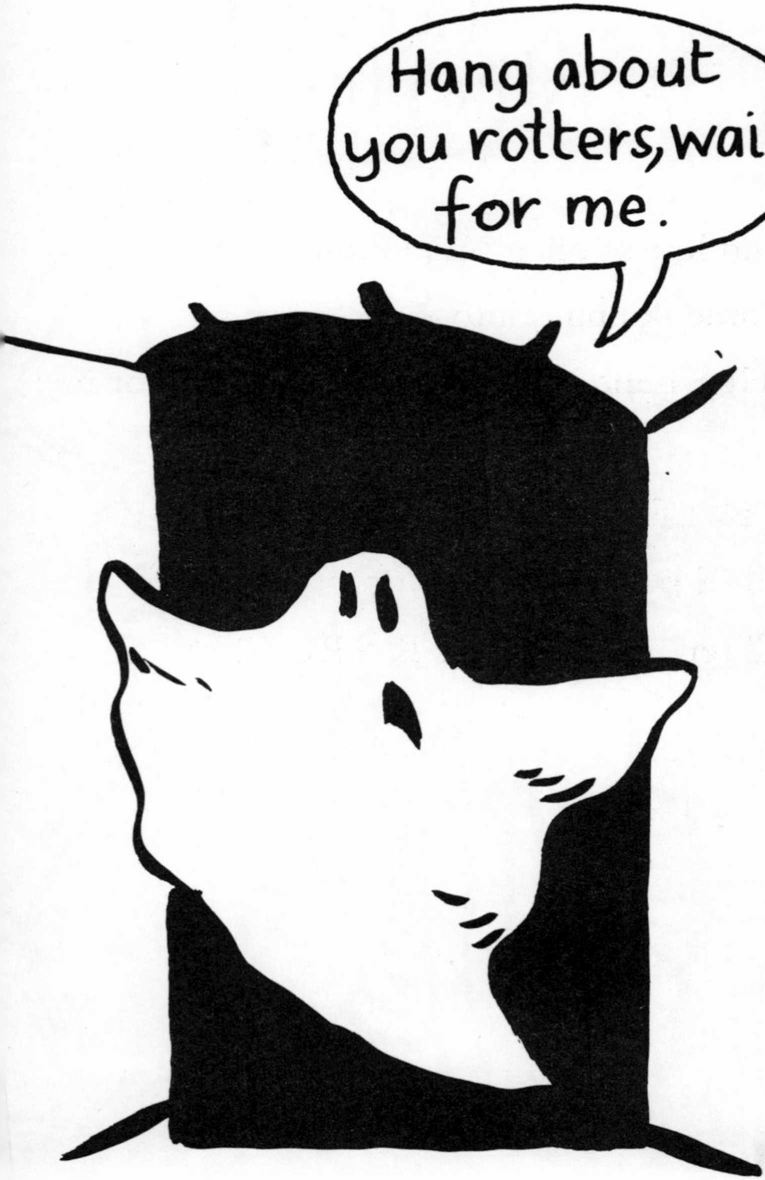
Hang about you rotters, wait for me.

"All right, gang," said the Skeleton,

"Now, here's the master scheme.

We have a go at everything in sight!

We'll try out every ride, and eat

A mountain of ice cream,

We're going to paint this fairground red

    tonight!"

"Quite right," agreed the Lady
With a sullen little pout,
"We've been stuck inside that train for
    weeks and weeks.

All that haunting's really daunting.
We deserve an evening out.
It'll put a bit of colour in our cheeks."

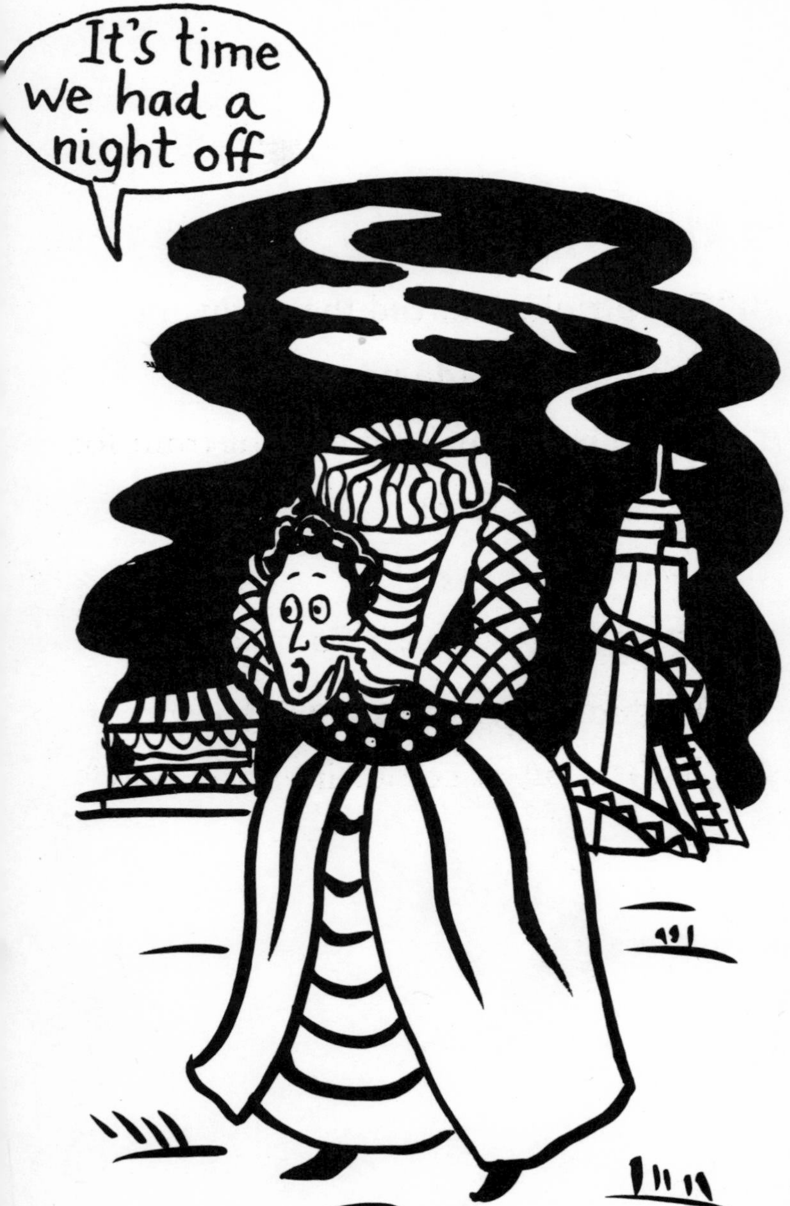
It's time we had a night off

"Let's start off with the Roundabout!"

The Mummy cried with glee,

"The Roundabout is always lots of fun!

Last one on's a cissy,

And I bet it won't be me!"

And he dashed across the fairground at

a run.

The Mummy chose a motorbike,

The Skeleton, a scooter,

The Lady chose a reindeer with a sleigh,

The Little Ghost decided

On a steam boat with a hooter

Which he honked in a relentless kind of way.

The Roundabout began to turn
And soon was spinning fast,
"Oh mercy!" wailed the Lady, "not so quick!"

They all felt rather dizzy
When they tumbled off at last,
And the Little Ghost complained of
feeling sick.

They took him to a soda stall.

He drank a fizzy drink

And got a lot of cuddles from the Mummy,

Then he ate six sticks of candyfloss,

All sugary and pink,

And declared he felt much better in his

tummy.

"I'm feeling in the mood for bumps,"
The Skeleton remarked,
"The Dodgem cars are parked just over here."

The Little Ghost responded
With excited little jumps,
And the others shouted gaily,
   "Good idea!"

30

They piled into the little cars
Of yellow, green and red,
And had a most exciting high speed chase,

And they had a lot of pile-ups
'Til the Lady lost her head,
And retired a little crossly from the race.

The Mummy saw the Hoopla Stall
And thought he'd try his luck, saying,
"Skill is what you need to throw this thing."

He won a little goldfish
And a yellow rubber duck,

And a hairy scary spider on a string!

Then the Lady won a coconut!
The others loudly cheered.
"Good shot, old girl," the Mummy
   proudly said.

"I'll carry it," the Skeleton

Politely volunteered,

"You've already got your hands full with
　your head."

40

Next they tried the swing boats
Where they really let off steam,
Up and down and to and fro they travelled.

The Little Ghost decided
It would scream and scream and SCREAM
And the Mummy got a tiny bit unravelled.

Then they tried the Helter Skelter

Which was quite a big success.

The Skeleton went backwards, for a dare.

He landed rather badly

In a jumbled, bony mess,

And it took a while to work out what

   went where.

They bought themselves some ice cream

And some burgers in a bun,

For the time had come to have a bite

to eat.

They sat upon the grass

And had a picnic (which was fun)

And the Little Ghost spilled ketchup down
his sheet.

And then – at last – the Ferris Wheel.
It rose into the sky,
Supported by a flimsy-looking frame.

"I'm frightened," said the Little Ghost.
"It looks so very high."
But he went and clambered on it just
the same.

They held each other tightly
As the giant wheel went round,
And everything beneath looked very smal

They screamed so very loudly
As they plunged towards the ground.
Said the Little Ghost, "I don't like this
at all."

But the view was most impressive
When they reached the very top.
Said the Lady, "This is really such a thrill!"

"Oh dear," remarked the Skeleton.
"I think it's time to stop.
The sun is coming up beyond the hill."

Sure enough, the sun was rising.

Very soon it would be dawn.

It was time to hurry back and board the
train.

"That was lovely," said the Little Ghost,
And added, with a yawn,
"Though I'm much too tired to do it all
again."

"What a night!" remarked the Skeleton.

"You're right," the others cried,

"It really has been such a lot of fun."

The carriage door swung open

And they tiredly climbed inside

(Not forgetting all the prizes they

    had won.)

That day, the poor old Ghost Train

Was sadly under-used.

All the passengers complained that it was

boring.

For instead of all the cackles

And the howlings and the boos . . .

There was nothing but the
sound of ghostly snoring!